Weekly Reader Books Presents

THE GRANDMA MIX-UP

story and pictures by
EMILY ARNOLD McCULLY

An I Can Read Book®

Harper & Row, Publishers

This book is a presentation of Weekly Reader Books.
Weekly Reader Books offers book clubs for children
from preschool through high school. For further
information write to: **Weekly Reader Books,**
4343 Equity Drive, Columbus, Ohio 43228.

Published by arrangement with Harper & Row, Publishers, Inc.
Weekly Reader is a federally registered trademark
of Field Publications.
I Can Read Book is a registered trademark of
Harper & Row, Publishers, Inc.

Library of Congress Cataloging-in-Publication Data
McCully, Emily Arnold.
  The grandma mix-up/by Emily Arnold McCully.—1st ed.
    p.   cm.   —   (An I can read book)
  Summary: Young Pip doesn't know what to do when two
very different grandmothers come to baby-sit, each with her
own way of doing things.
  ISBN 0-06-024201-9 : $
  ISBN 0-06-024202-7 (lib. bdg.) : $
  [1. Babysitters—Fiction.   2. Grandmothers—Fiction.]
I. Title.   II. Series.
PZ7.M478415Gr 1988   87-29378
[E]—dc19   CIP
                                                    AC

For Penny MacDonald and Em Brinkley

1 THE MIX-UP

Pip's mom and dad
were taking a trip.

"We will be gone

two days and two nights,"

said Pip's mom.

"Grandma Nan

will take care of you."

Mom and Dad and Pip

went downstairs

to wait for Grandma Nan.

"Here she comes!" cried Pip.

"Hi, Grandma Nan!"

"Hello, hello," said Grandma Nan.

"How is my good grandchild?"

11

Just then

a taxi raced up.

Out popped Grandma Sal.

"Here I am," she called.

"Did you ask Grandma Sal to baby-sit?"

Mom asked Dad.

"Did you ask Grandma Nan to baby-sit?"

Dad asked Mom.

"Now what will we do?"

"No matter," said Grandma Sal.

"We can both baby-sit!"

"Are you sure?" asked Dad.

"Run along," said Grandma Sal.

"We will have a fine time."

"Good-bye, Pip," said Dad.

"We will miss you," said Mom.

16

They hugged Pip good-bye
and rode away in a taxi.

2 A BAD START

"Well!" said Grandma Nan.

"Let's get busy!"

"Let's relax!"

said Grandma Sal.

"Open your treat bag, Pip."

"Gummy Bears," said Pip.

"Thank you!"

"Come upstairs,"

said Grandma Nan.

"First thing in the morning,

I inspect your room."

20

Pip followed her upstairs.

"Oh, Pip," said Grandma Nan sadly.

"Our room is a mess!

We must clean it up!"

Pip put away the socks

and trucks and crayons,

and pulled up the bed covers.

Grandma Nan was very strict!

"Pip, Pip!" called Grandma Sal

from the backyard.

"Come down

and show me your bike!"

23

Pip ran outside.

"Look at you!"

said Grandma Sal.

"You are a super-duper rider!"

"Hi-ho," called Grandma Nan.

"It is noon on the dot.

Time to eat lunch."

Pip and Grandma Sal went inside.

"You may have tuna with sprouts,"

said Grandma Nan.

"Or an apple, some nuts,
a marshmallow, cereal, pretzels,
or corned-beef hash,"
said Grandma Sal.

It was too hard to choose.

"I'm not hungry," Pip said.

"Oh, dear. I don't like

the sound of that,"

said Grandma Nan.

"Maybe a nap is in order."

28

"You bet your life!"

said Grandma Sal.

She plopped down

onto the couch.

"See you later, Pip."

3 WORSE AND WORSE

"Rise and shine!"

called Grandma Nan.

"Nap time is over.

We want to be busy now!"

"What do we want to do?"

asked Pip.

"Oh, paint us a picture,"

said Grandma Nan.

"Or act out a story...

or do a puzzle...."

31

Grandma Sal was in the living room.

"The big game is on TV,"

she said.

"Want to watch?

Want a chip?"

"I think I will go

back upstairs," said Pip.

Pip sat down

to write a secret letter.

"Dear Mom and Dad,

Grandma Nan is too hard,

and Grandma Sal is too easy.

I want you to come home

and do things our way.

Love, Pip."

Pip put the letter
into the desk drawer
and went out front
to sit on the steps.

"Dinner time!"

called Grandma Nan.

"Please set the table."

Grandma Nan was stirring a big pot.

"Stew!" she said.

"If it stinks," said Grandma Sal,

"we can send out for pizza."

Pip ate one bite of stew

to be polite.

"Pip," said Grandma Nan,

"we must eat to be strong."

"Now, Nan," said Grandma Sal,

"the child will not starve."

"May I go outside?"

asked Pip.

"If you keep clean,"

said Grandma Nan.

40

"Pip can always take a bath,"

said Grandma Sal.

Both grandmas were grumpy.

4 DOING THINGS PIP'S WAY

Pip went outside

to swing high on the swing.

Grandma Nan wanted

to do things one way,

and Grandma Sal wanted

to do things another way.

Pip wanted to do things

the way Mom and Dad and Pip

always did them.

The grandmas were talking

by the window.

"A child needs rules, Sal,"

said Grandma Nan.

"A child needs fun, Nan,"

said Grandma Sal.

"My rule is bed at 8 o'clock,"

said Grandma Nan.

"Oh, loosen up,"

said Grandma Sal.

"A body gets

the sleep it needs."

"STOP!" cried Pip.

"I do not want

to do everything two ways.

I want to do them *our* way,

like every day

when Mom and Dad are home."

"How is that, dear?"

asked Grandma Nan.

"I clean up my room

once a week.

I make my own lunch

every day.

I don't take a nap

unless I want to,

and I never have candy

in the morning

except at Christmas.

No TV on nice days,

and I can get dirty when I play.

And I don't eat vegetables

all mixed up with meat."

"What do you think, Sal?"

asked Grandma Nan.

"The child has a point,"

said Grandma Sal.

"Pip, we will try

to do things your way,"

said Grandma Nan.

"How do we begin?"

"It is almost my bedtime,"

said Pip.

"But first

I put on my pajamas,

and then I brush my teeth

and pet kitty

and wash my face.

Then I look out for stars

and eat a cookie

and run my trucks,

and then I bounce on my bed

if I feel like it.

Then you can read me a story."

"Oh, goody, a story,"

said Grandma Nan.

She reached for the bookshelf.

"Oh, goody," said Grandma Sal.

She reached into her bag.

"Oh, no," said Pip.

"*I* choose the book.

It is upstairs.

You can take turns reading it."

Pip got ready for bed.

The grandmas waited.

After a while,

Grandma Nan called up,

"It's getting late, Pip!"

"Relax, Nan," said Grandma Sal.

The grandmas laughed.

Finally

Pip crawled under the covers.

Then Grandma Nan

read the first page,

and Grandma Sal

read the next page

of Pip's bedtime book.

They took turns

to the very end.

After that,

the grandmas

did almost everything

Pip's way—

until Pip's mom and dad

came home.